The Terrific Talent Show

The Aristokittens

Welcome to the Creature Café
The Great Biscuit Bake-Off
The Fantastic Rabbit Race

DISNEY

The Terrific Talent Show

By Jennifer Castle

Illustrated by Sydney Hanson

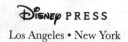

DISNEY PRESS

Los Angeles • New York

Printed in the United States of America

First Paperback Edition, August 2023

1 3 5 7 9 10 8 6 4 2

ISBN 978-1-368-09370-5
FAC-004510-23180

Library of Congress Control Number: 2023934144

Book design by Emily Fisher

Visit disneybooks.com

SUSTAINABLE FORESTRY INITIATIVE

Certified Sourcing

www.forests.org
SFI-01681

Logo Applies to Text Stock Only

Chapter 1

Marie couldn't believe her eyes.

Her brother Toulouse. Napping in a spot of sunlight on the upstairs hallway floor. Curled into a ball of orange fur, like a little pumpkin.

"Wow," Marie's other brother, Berlioz, whispered over her shoulder. "He's actually asleep."

Toulouse almost *never* took a nap. He was always going, going, going. But it had been a busy week at the Purrfect

Paw-tisserie, the animal café Marie and her brothers ran. Today was Monday, when the café was closed. An idea popped into Marie's head.

"Berlioz," she said. "Remember the other morning, when Toulouse woke you and me up by sitting on us? We should give him a taste of his own medicine."

Berlioz purred and thumped his gray tail against the floor. "Yes! You pounce on his head. I'll jump on his back."

Marie and Berlioz leapt at the same time.

"MROWWW!" Toulouse howled as his littermates landed on him. "I'm going to get you for that! I was having the best dream!"

"You'll have to catch us first!" Marie called.

She darted away. The big house they lived in with their human, Madame Adelaide Bonfamille, had many rooms where Marie could find a place to hide. As she ran, she looked for an open door. But they were all closed . . . except one. *Aha!*

Then she realized which door it was and froze.

She'd never, ever seen this door open before. Their mama, Duchess, had made the kittens promise to never go through it. She'd told them the staircase inside that door led to a dirty, dusty, and possibly dangerous place:

The attic.

The *pitter-pat* of Toulouse's paws sounded down the hallway. Maybe Marie could hide behind the door.

She squeezed through the opening. *I won't go farther than this.*

But then came the smells, wafting down from the top of the staircase. So many interesting scents! Marie climbed onto the first step to get a better whiff. It creaked loudly.

"Aha!" Toulouse exclaimed as he peeked around the door. "I knew I heard something. Oh! Are these the attic stairs? Marie, you'd better come back down. You remember what Mama said about—"

"I know," Marie told him. "But haven't you always been curious?" She climbed another step. "What is that smell? And that one? And that other one?"

Toulouse took three quick sniffs. His tail whipped back and forth. "I don't know. But I, uh, think I have to find out."

He started to follow Marie.

"Marie! Toulouse!" Berlioz appeared in the doorway, shaking his head. "You're going to get us in so much trouble!"

"Come on, Berlioz," Toulouse called from halfway up the staircase. Marie was nearly at the top now. "We'll just take a peek. Don't you want to know what's up here?"

Berlioz's nose twitched. "It does smell . . . fascinating. But what if there are huge bats everywhere?"

"*Pffft,*" Toulouse said. "Thomas O'Malley says bats are just mice with wings."

CRRRRRREAKKKKK. A noise came from above them.

"Or there could be a *ghost* . . ." Toulouse muttered.

Marie climbed another step. "Good thing I don't believe in ghosts," she said, but puffed herself up. Just in case she needed to look big and scary. Then Marie crouched down and leapt up the rest of the way.

She was officially in the attic now. Giant shadows flickered across the walls. Cobwebs hung from the ceiling. Duchess was right: this place might give her nightmares!

Then Marie's eyes adjusted to the darkness. "Oh my gosh," she whispered.

In every corner, the things Marie saw were not spooky and scary, but strange and wonderful: A velvet chair with only one arm. A bicycle covered in rust. A huge table placed upside down so the legs stood like four towers. Stacks of wooden boxes. And against a wall, a big metal trunk with a key in the lock.

"Is it safe?" Berlioz called from the staircase.

"What's up there?" Toulouse added.

"Come see for yourselves!" Marie replied.

Toulouse and Berlioz both landed at the top of the stairs and skidded to a stop.

"Oooh," Berlioz murmured. "So many boxes. I . . . love . . . boxes."

Marie headed for the locked trunk. Anything behind a key had to be worth exploring!

"I'm going to try to get this open," she said. "If I stand on something and stretch up with my paws, I can reach."

"How about these?" Toulouse asked, nudging at a pile of books with his nose. Once he pushed them close enough to the chest, Marie hopped on top. She batted at the key with one paw. Once, twice, then finally, on the third try . . . the key turned. The chest popped open to reveal colors: purple, blue, pink. Lots of sparkle and shine. Clothing decorated with gems, feathers, and ribbons.

"These must be Madame's old

costumes," Marie said, sniffing at a red velvet cape with jeweled buttons.

"I think you're right," Berlioz added. "I recognize that cape from a portrait of Madame downstairs."

Duchess had told them many tales about Madame's years as an opera star. An opera, their mama had explained, was a very dramatic play where the story was told by singing songs instead of talking. Madame would sing onstage for big audiences, playing all sorts of interesting characters. To Marie, that sounded like a dream come true.

Toulouse spotted another trunk and bounded over to it. "Let's see what's in this one."

When they got that trunk open, Toulouse let out an excited *"Meow!"* The chest was full of hats, gloves, handbags, scarves, and even a few pairs of spectacles. Toulouse leapt into the trunk and started to dig.

"I love accessories!" he exclaimed. "They're so *artistic*."

Toulouse popped his head out of the pile. He was wearing a big black hat, a pair of spectacles, and a flowered scarf around his neck.

"Bonjour," he said, in a deep, silly voice. "Today I am going to model the latest Paris fashions for you."

Then he did a fancy walk past Marie, crossing one paw in front of the other, swishing his tail in a little circle. Marie burst out laughing.

"Hey, look at these!" Berlioz called, standing near an overturned wooden box. Dozens of papers, covered in black lines and dots and scribbles, had spilled onto the floor. Marie recognized them as sheet music. From her time learning scales and arpeggios with her brothers, she knew these notes made up songs. Often there were lyrics, too.

"Do you know any of these songs?" Marie asked Berlioz. "'Flower Duet'? 'Musetta's Waltz'?"

 11

"No," Berlioz replied. "They must be from old operas."

Marie shuffled through the sheets of paper, trying to read lyrics written in faded pencil. A few words from one song jumped out at her.

As winter steps aside for spring
All the earth begins to sing
Wrapped in green grass and rainbow
   flowers
Thank you to Nature's magic powers

"Hmmm, that's an interesting melody," Berlioz said, looking over Marie's shoulder. He started to hum as he read the notes.

"It sounds so pretty," Marie said.

"Try to sing along," Berlioz
suggested.

Berlioz hummed the melody
again, and Marie started singing the lyrics.

Toulouse, now wearing a tall red top
hat, climbed onto a dresser. He took off
the hat and waved it around, dancing to
the song.

Marie smiled as she sang. She loved
it when she, Berlioz, and Toulouse all
performed together . . . even if there
was no audience. Even if they were just
having fun.

"HELLO?"

It was Madame's voice, coming from
the hallway below them.

"My darling kittens, where are you?"

Marie, Berlioz, and Toulouse all

froze. They glanced nervously at one another. What would happen if Madame found them up here?

CRREAKKK.

Marie heard the door open, and footsteps on the attic stairs.

"Oh, my!" she heard Madame exclaim. "I must have left this door open last night. I hope the kittens didn't wander up there."

Marie's whiskers trembled. She never, ever wanted to make Madame angry with her. Or even disappointed. Madame would be both when she found they'd been playing with her belongings. Then Duchess would know they'd broken the rules.

MRRRROW.

The noise came from the hallway,

too. Marie would recognize the voice of her stepdad, Thomas O'Malley, anywhere.

MEEEE-ROWWWWW.

Madame laughed. "Hello, Monsieur Thomas! You're asking so politely for attention. How can I refuse?"

Thomas O'Malley let out some happy little meows. Madame was probably scratching him under his chin, one of his favorite things in the world.

Marie sighed with relief. Had their stepdad distracted Madame on purpose?

"Ah, so Madame was right," said a voice.

Their mama, Duchess, perched on the attic landing, her ears back, tapping her tail on the floor.

"I wanted to find you before Madame did," she continued. "Don't you remember what I said about the attic?"

"It's dirty and dusty," Marie mumbled.

"And possibly dangerous," Berlioz added.

"Yes," said Duchess. "But most importantly, everything up here is special to Madame. Now here you are, going through her belongings without permission."

"We're sorry," Marie said. "We were just so curious and then, the smells! Old wood and paper and perfume . . ."

"And all these boxes and chests that needed to be opened!" Toulouse explained.

"We promise it won't happen again," Berlioz said, hanging his head.

 17

Duchess nodded, and Berlioz and Toulouse began cleaning up. Toulouse took off his hat and put it neatly in the trunk. Berlioz scooped the sheet music back into the box.

Duchess turned to Marie. "Marie, aren't you going to help your brothers put things back where you found them?"

Marie looked down at the sheet music. Singing those notes and words had made her so happy. She wanted to learn the whole song, then sing it again and again.

"No," Marie blurted out.

Surprised, Duchess flattened her ears. "No, you're not going to help?"

Marie shook her head. "I mean, no, I don't want to put this music back. I want to keep it."

Chapter 2

Duchess blinked her sapphire-blue eyes at her daughter. "Keep it?" she echoed, confused.

"Would that be okay, Mama?" Marie asked in her most polite voice. "Just for a little while?"

Duchess blinked again. "May I ask why?"

"I, um . . . would like to perform it. Maybe at the café, with Berlioz."

"Perform it . . ." Duchess

repeated. Her expression grew soft and dreamy.

"Mama?" Toulouse asked. "Are you going to say *yes*?"

Marie swatted at him. "Shhhh. Can't you see she's thinking about it?"

Duchess finally smiled at Marie.

"I was about your age when I first heard Madame sing," Duchess told her. Berlioz and Toulouse drew close so they could listen, too. "Oh, her voice was so beautiful. It was as if . . . the music made my heart dance."

"I know that feeling, Mama," Berlioz said.

"I'm sure you do, my darling," Duchess replied, giving him a quick nuzzle. "From that moment on, music was part of my life. I heard rhythms and melodies everywhere! Not just from Madame, but when the birds chirped. When the Paris church bells rang. Even when horses trotted down the street. Then you were born, kittens. That's why I taught you scales and arpeggios as soon as you were old enough."

"But, Mama," Toulouse murmured, "Berlioz and Marie are much better at making music than I am."

Duchess smiled at him. "That's because something else makes your heart dance: art. Art is your talent. The gift you share with the world. Everybody has one." She paused, lost in her thoughts, then continued. "I must admit, it would be quite wonderful to hear one of Madame's old songs again."

"Is that a yes?" Marie asked, trying to hide her excitement.

"Yes," Duchess replied. "But you are just *borrowing* this sheet music. Please take good care of it."

"I will! I will! Thank you, Mama!" Marie gently picked up the sheet music with her teeth and hurried toward the stairs. She needed to get to the piano. Berlioz and Toulouse raced after her, out of the attic and down the hall. As they passed Madame's bedroom, Marie glimpsed Madame sitting in a chair with Thomas O'Malley curled up asleep in her lap.

Marie and her brothers zipped down the grand staircase. The door to Alley Cat Parlor, a room where all the street cats of Paris were welcome to live, was ajar.

Berlioz peeked in. "The piano's free. Come on."

The kittens scurried into the strangely quiet parlor. Usually, cats of all breeds, sizes, and colors filled this room. They'd bat toys around, tussle on the floor, and often play music.

But now, Marie saw only a gray-and-white-striped cat napping on a sofa.

"Where is everyone?" Toulouse whispered.

"Probably out exploring," Berlioz replied with a shrug. "It's trash day, remember?"

"Perfect for us," Marie said after she hopped onto the piano stool and put the papers on the music rack. Berlioz hopped up, too, and stretched out his claws one by one. In the past, this had always annoyed Marie. But now, she used those moments to warm up her own voice.

"Mee, may, mah, moh, moo," Marie sang.

Toulouse scrambled onto the stool with them so he could be the sheet music page turner.

"Ready?" Marie asked her brothers.

"On three," Berlioz replied.

He counted, then began playing. Marie thought it was amazing that

Berlioz could learn music so quickly. She took a deep breath and opened her mouth to sing.

Suddenly, a *MRROWWW!* came out of nowhere. Startled, Berlioz played a bunch of wrong notes that hurt Marie's ears. A furry orange-and-white-striped face popped up from behind the piano.

"Oh, hello, Henri!" Toulouse exclaimed. "We didn't know you were sleeping back there."

"Humph," Henri grumbled, blinking heavily. "This is my secret napping spot, between the piano and the window. It's always nice and warm." He paused, then added, "Don't tell anyone about it."

"We're sorry we woke you up," Berlioz offered.

"Humph," Henri said again.

"Well, at least you woke me with a nice song."

"It's one of Madame's old songs," Marie told him.

Henri nodded, then quickly disappeared behind the piano. Marie shot a confused look at her brothers. Henri then stepped out from his secret space, holding a violin.

"May I play along?" he asked.

All three kittens replied with a chorus of "Yes!"

They started the song again from the beginning. Now, with the violin, it sounded even more beautiful. Marie threw herself into the lyrics, thinking how music made her heart dance, the same way it did Mama's.

A moment later, something else was

happening. A new sound in the song. Low, but sweet. Marie turned to see the gray-and-white-striped cat from the sofa, Isabel, standing next to Henri—playing a clarinet!

Marie noticed a shape dart out from beneath a chair: a black-and-white tuxedo cat named Antonio. As Marie sang and everyone else played, Antonio danced gracefully around the room. His tuxedo markings made him look like some of the other opera singers in Madame's old photos.

Everyone has their own talent, Marie thought, remembering what Duchess had said.

In that instant, an idea hit Marie so hard, she stopped singing. Luckily, they were almost at the end of the song.

When Berlioz was done playing, he, Toulouse, Henri, Isabel, and Antonio all stared at her.

"Marie, are you okay?" Berlioz asked.

"A talent show!" she exclaimed, jumping from the piano stool to the arm of a chair. "What if we had a talent show at the Purrfect Paw-tisserie? Our friends and customers could sign up to perform!"

Berlioz and Toulouse stared at her. Their whiskers quivered. Their ears twitched. Marie could tell they were thinking about it.

"I would love a chance to play the clarinet at your café," Isabel said, her green eyes blazing with excitement.

"And I've never danced for an

29

audience," Antonio added. "But I've, um, always wanted to."

"Great!" Marie told him. Another idea popped into her head. "I'd sing this song, of course, but I could also be the director. Every show needs one."

Berlioz and Toulouse frowned.

"What would *we* do?" Berlioz asked.

"You can do an act, too," Marie replied. "And play piano for any performers who need music. Then Toulouse . . ."

Marie took a few moments to think. They could make a little stage in the café, with a backdrop.

"Toulouse, you could be the set designer," Marie finally said.

Toulouse broke into a big smile. "I'm just the cat for that job."

"Would we help you run the show, too?" Berlioz asked. "The way we do with the café?"

"Yes, of course!" Marie replied. "We could all be co-directors. There will be lots of work and organizing to do. It's better if there are three of us."

"Work?" Toulouse asked with a yawn.

Berlioz's whiskers drooped. "Organizing?"

"Of course," Marie said matter-of-factly. "Let's have a brainstorming session."

Toulouse yawned again. "Can't we just share our ideas whenever we think of them?"

No! Marie thought, a little annoyed. *We need to plan ahead for something like a*

talent show. Before she had a chance to say this, someone else spoke up.

"Ah, we used to put on shows all the time at the Café des Creatures."

Marie glanced over to the kitchen door to see that her baking instructor, a fluffy black cat named Louis, had been listening to all these plans. He'd run the café years ago along with their French bulldog friend Pierre.

"You'll need hosts, too," Louis went on. "To introduce each act."

"We could take turns doing that," Toulouse offered, his eyes lighting up. "Right, Marie?"

"Absolutely!" Marie replied. "We can write out scripts for what we'll say."

"Or we could just make it up as we go along . . ." Berlioz suggested.

 32

To Marie, that sounded like a terrible idea. An idea that would lead to a lot of problems. Knowing her and her brothers, a lot of arguing, too. How could she explain that to them? Right now, everyone was so excited, chatting about what acts they wanted to do. But surely she'd have time to talk to them later. They'd understand why it was important to have a plan.

Marie started to feel as excited as everyone else. She closed her eyes and imagined singing Madame's song on a stage at the Paw-tisserie. Mama would be watching, of course, and looking so proud.

This show was going to be terrific!

Chapter 3

*W*ow, Marie thought. *Mama was right. Everyone truly does have their own talent.*

So many friends had signed up for the Purrfect Paw-tisserie's first Terrific Talent Show. For everyone to fit inside the café, the kittens rearranged the tables and formed a big circle of chairs. Marie made sure the café customers had what they needed, then sat down next to their friend Pouf the squirrel.

He started poking her with his little paws.

"Did I tell you about my act?" he asked. "Did I? I did, right? Wait until you see me juggle acorns. I've been practicing my whole life!"

"You told me," Marie said, smiling at the thought. This was exactly the kind of talent show act she'd imagined.

"That's not even the best part! After I juggle, I'm going to break my own personal record for how many acorns I can stuff in my cheeks!"

Pouf held up a little brown sack, grabbed an acorn from inside, and stuffed it in his right cheek. He put the next acorn in his left cheek. Two more acorns, one on each side. His cheeks puffed out like little balloons.

"Sheeeeeee howwwww grrrrrrreatttttt I ammmmm," Pouf mumbled, reaching for another acorn.

"Pouf!" Marie said, holding up a paw. "You don't have to do your whole act right now. Thank you for the sneak peek, though."

Pouf stared at her for a moment, then nodded. He sat back down but left the acorns in his cheeks.

"Please don't put me on right after Pouf," a tiny voice squeaked from a chair across the circle. It was Spike the hedgehog, who'd recently shared one of his talents by winning the café's Dog Biscuit Bake-Off.

"What kind of performance would you like to do?" Berlioz asked his friend.

Spike smiled, but in a shy way. "Well, sometimes I do this little trick, and my mother always said it was very entertaining. It's easier if I show you."

The hedgehog jumped onto the floor and curled up into a little ball of spiky-looking fur. Marie couldn't see his head or feet. Then, Spike slowly rolled inside the chair circle—first in a straight line, then in a pattern. His rolling grew faster. And faster! Spike sped up even more, whizzing by everyone. It made Marie dizzy just to watch.

Finally, he stopped, and everyone burst into applause.

"Spike, that was fantastic!" Marie said.

Spike unrolled himself and took a little bow. "Berlioz, would you play some music to go with my rolling?"

"Of course!" Berlioz told him.

"Are *you* going to do an act?" the hedgehog asked Berlioz.

"Oh, yes," Berlioz replied. "I'm practicing a jazz number with some of the cats from Alley Cat Parlor, like Isabel."

Isabel sat nearby, holding her clarinet in one paw and a kitty croissant in the other.

"Here's a sample," Isabel said,

swallowing the last of her croissant.
Then she readied her clarinet and started
playing a bouncy tune, full of energy.
Marie couldn't hear jazz music without
moving in some way. She swished her
tail and bobbed her head. Pouf, Spike,
and Toulouse hopped off their chairs and
started dancing in the middle of the circle.

This is so silly, Marie thought. *And
fun. I love it!*

When the song was done and
everyone had applauded, Antonio
the tuxedo cat told them he was
choreographing a dance for the show.

Then Toulouse spoke up. "Pierre
told me that when they used to put on
shows here, he would tell funny jokes
onstage. He's been teaching them to me.
I was thinking I could do that as my act."

"That sounds perfect, Toulouse," Marie said. "Today after the café closes, we should decide what order the acts should be in."

Toulouse flattened his ears. "Why do we need to put them in order ahead of time? It would be more fun if it was all random. We could write down the performers' names, and to decide who goes next, we'd pull one out of a hat."

Berlioz giggled. "I like that idea! It'll make the show exciting."

Marie frowned and shook her head. "But the show will already be exciting, because the *acts* will be exciting. A real performance has everything planned out ahead of time. The order of the acts, the music, even what we'll say as the hosts."

"But that's so boring . . ." Toulouse

said with a groan, rolling his eyes. "I was planning on just making up what I say as we go along."

"It's not boring," Marie said, starting to feel frustrated. "It's theater. It's how things are supposed to be done."

"This isn't some fancy opera house, though," Berlioz said. "It's a talent show at a secret creature café!"

Marie let out a little growl. She glanced away from her annoying brothers, fighting the urge to give them a long, loud hiss.

She spotted a calico kitty waiting patiently at the counter to order. They couldn't ignore a new guest.

"I think that's enough planning for today," she announced to everyone in the circle. "My brothers and I will talk more later. Right now, we need to get back to work."

Marie hurried behind the bakery counter. Her head was swimming. How could she help Berlioz and Toulouse understand how important this was to her? She really wanted to do something that was good, not just *good enough*. And that meant being organized.

"I'm sorry to keep you waiting," Marie said to the calico kitty, who had white fur like Marie's own but with orange and gray patches. She looked older than a kitten but younger than the grown-up cats. Marie admired the kitty's hat: it was purple, with a round brim. She wore a matching scarf around her neck. "How can I help you?"

"I'd love to try one of those mini quiches," the calico said. She spoke with a posh accent, like Madame's human friends from England. Marie always thought they sounded like kings and queens. The kitty then leaned across the counter and dropped her voice to a whisper. "Also, I couldn't help overhearing you and those other two kittens."

Marie glanced at Berlioz and Toulouse, who'd started chasing each other around the circle of chairs.

"My brothers," Marie said, and rolled her eyes.

"Well," the kitty began, "I agree with you. My family and I live with a human theater troupe. Believe me, when it comes to putting on a show, you absolutely must have some kind of plan."

Marie's ears tilted forward. "Did you say you *live* with a theater troupe?"

The kitty nodded, then smiled. "Yes. In London. I'm Daisy. Sorry, I should have introduced myself right away. This is my first trip away from home on my own, and I've been a little nervous."

"Hi, Daisy. My name's Marie. There's a free table in the corner, over there. Have a seat and I'll bring you your order."

A few minutes later, Marie sat at the table with Daisy as the calico enjoyed her mini quiche and some lavender tea with cream.

"Wow," Marie said, fascinated. "A trip away from home by yourself. I can't even imagine." She glanced over at Berlioz and Toulouse. "Although sometimes when my brothers are being extra annoying, I find someplace else to be. Away from them."

Daisy giggled. "I understand. I was so happy when the troupe wanted to bring one of us when they came to perform in Paris. They say it's good luck to have a cat at the theater!"

Marie thought back to the argument with Toulouse and Berlioz. "So you think I'm right, that we have to be organized about our talent show? Not just make things up as we go along?"

"Absolutely," Daisy said. "Set up an order of the acts ahead of time, and write out what the host says. That way, you can rehearse it before the show. That's what real theater folks do."

Marie couldn't believe it: someone

who understood her. And not just any someone, but a teenage kitty from London. *Maybe this is what it's like to have a big sister.*

"I have to admit," Marie began, feeling like she could really open up to Daisy, "I'm so excited, but also very nervous. I can see the whole show in my head. Especially the song I want to perform. But what if the actual show doesn't match what I'm imagining?"

Daisy thought for a moment. "Well . . . in the theater, nobody works alone. You'll need others to help you make your show a success."

Marie sighed. "I'm not sure I can count on Toulouse and Berlioz to do that." Marie had a sudden brainstorm. "Wait! Daisy, would *you* want to help?

You're an expert. Would you want to be my assistant director?"

Daisy leapt off her chair and onto the floor. Marie could hear her start to purr. "I would love that!"

"It's a plan!" Marie said.

Then she spotted Berlioz standing nearby. From the hurt look on his face, Marie could tell he'd heard that last part of the conversation. Her brother dropped his head and slinked to the other side of the café.

I didn't mean to hurt his feelings, Marie thought.

And Berlioz and Toulouse had acted like they didn't want to be co-directors anyway.

This would be best for everyone.

Chapter 4

"It's right around this corner," Daisy told Marie.

Marie followed her new friend down a busy Paris street, into an unfamiliar neighborhood. After meeting Daisy, her mama had been happy to give permission for this "educational" outing. They scurried past outdoor cafés that smelled like coffee, honey, and chocolate, and crossed through a public square, where children played around a fountain.

Daisy rounded a corner and stopped at a lamppost, staring up at something with a smile. "Ta-da! There it is!"

Marie caught up to Daisy, unsure what to expect.

Oh my gosh.

The building stood back from the street, stone columns decorating its front. Wide stone steps led up to the entrance. A huge sign above it read *Le Théâtre du Lion Jaune*. The Yellow Lion Theater.

"A real professional theater," Marie said with a sigh. "Mama said Madame used to perform here."

"Wait until you see the inside," Daisy told her. "Come on!"

She led Marie alongside the building to a half-open basement window.

They squeezed through and landed on a bookshelf in an office. From the bookshelf, they jumped to the floor. Ran out of the office and down a hallway. Raced up a flight of steps.

At the top of the steps, a human swept the floors, humming to himself. Marie felt nervous, but the man waved when he saw them.

"Hello there, Daisy," he said with a bright smile. "Oh! You've got a friend today!"

Mrrrowww, Daisy responded. Marie meowed, too, to be polite.

Daisy led Marie to a pair of huge wooden doors. She meowed at the human.

"Yes, yes, of course, Mademoiselle Daisy," he said, laughing. "At your service."

The man pulled one of the doors open for them.

"They just do whatever you want them to?" Marie mumbled to Daisy.

Daisy laughed. "Most of the time. If I ask nicely and make a cute face. Come on, we're almost there."

Marie followed Daisy through the door . . . then froze in disbelief.

It was like she'd stepped into another world.

Rows and rows of red velvet seats stretched out in front of Marie. Above her head, there were balconies draped in gold fabric, with more red velvet seats inside them. The ceiling was painted with a mural of blue sky and white clouds. And then, at the center of it all:

the stage, framed with a giant red-and-gold velvet curtain.

"Would you like a closer look?" Daisy asked. Marie nodded. "Then come with me. Quick, before the troupe starts rehearsal."

Moments later, Marie stood on the stage. She'd never felt so big. Her heart raced. Or was it dancing? She gazed out at all those red velvet seats and imagined them filled with her family and friends. Duchess and Thomas O'Malley, along with her brothers, would be in the front row.

Marie's imaginary audience also included Pierre, Louis, Pouf, Spike, and many other animals she'd met since opening the Paw-tisserie: the puppies Claudette, Nadine, and Leon, and Angelique the racing rabbit.

She pictured herself singing Madame's springtime song. Finishing up that last, long note. Everyone bursting into applause. Giving her a standing ovation, even! Marie took a little bow before she realized this was all happening in a daydream.

"You're just like me," Daisy said with a smile. "I love being onstage, too. Even if nobody's in the audience."

"It's all so . . . magical," Marie sighed.

"Come on, I'll show you what's behind the magic."

Daisy led Marie to an area just off the stage, behind another curtain. "These are called the wings," Daisy told her. "There's one on each side."

From there, Daisy took Marie on

a tour of all the parts of a theater. The backdrops were called scenery flats. There was a big box of things called props, objects that would be used in the show—a book, an empty sack, a ball. They climbed halfway up a ladder so Daisy could show Marie all the different lights hanging from the ceiling.

Then came Marie's favorite part: the costume department, a room filled with the most wonderful fabrics and colors . . . and, of course, smells. Toulouse would have loved it here! Daisy wrapped herself in the bottom of a flowered dress that was hanging on a rack.

"Hello," she said in a fancy voice. "My name is . . . Petunia Picklebottom, and I'd like to invite you to tea at the most amazing creature café in Paris!"

Marie giggled. "Hello, Petunia!"

Daisy became Daisy again. "If you could choose any of these costumes to wear for the talent show, which would you pick?"

Marie scanned all the clothing, sniffing the air in case something stood out to her. Across the room, she spotted a pink silk dress that perfectly matched her bow. She ran over to it, wrapped herself in the bottom, and poked her head out.

She then started to sing one of her family's favorite songs, about how everyone wanted to be a cat.

After Marie sang a few lines, Daisy thumped her tail on the floor and exclaimed, "Brava! Brava!"

Marie bowed, and both cats laughed.

"We still have to see the best part," Daisy said. She led Marie into one of the dressing rooms. Marie nearly gasped when she saw the huge mirror framed with bright lights.

Daisy leapt onto the table in front of the mirror. "This is where the performers get ready. It's when all the rehearsals are done, and you have a moment before you go onstage. To just . . . feel happy and excited."

Marie jumped up to join Daisy. They both stared into the mirror. Daisy leaned her head in close to Marie's, as if they were posing for a picture.

"Look at us," Daisy said. "Two future stars."

Marie was struck with an idea. "I can't believe I didn't think of this

before," she said. "But . . . would you like to do an act in the talent show?"

Daisy's eyes grew wide. "Oh my gosh, yes! I was feeling too shy to ask."

"Too shy?" Marie echoed. *"You?"*

Daisy shrugged. "Like I said, I get a little nervous, being on a trip without my family. But I *have* been working on something I'd love to perform. You see, there's a play by a famous English playwright, William Shakespeare, called *Romeo and Juliet.* It's about two humans who fall in love, but their families are enemies. I wrote my own version, *Ro-meow and Julie-cat.*"

"It sounds very dramatic," Marie said.

"Oh, it is! There's this one part where Julie-cat is talking alone on the stage. That's called a monologue. It would be perfect for me to perform as the final act in the talent show."

Marie felt her stomach drop. *But I imagined MY song to be the final act.*

"It's always been my dream to close a show," Daisy continued. "Every time I see the humans do it, they get so much applause!"

Marie nodded, not sure what to say.

"And I had another idea," Daisy added. "Your song would be great for *opening* the show. The first act needs to have a lot of energy."

Marie could see Daisy's excitement for these ideas. Her new friend had already been so nice: agreeing to be assistant director, giving her this special backstage tour. Plus, Daisy knew all about putting on a show, and Marie was new to it. *Maybe Daisy's right. Maybe my song should be the first act, not the last.*

"I agree completely," Marie said.

Chapter 5

The day before the talent show's scheduled performance, the kittens held one last rehearsal.

Marie, Toulouse, and Berlioz worked at the café all morning to create the stage. They took six of the shortest tables and pushed them together to make a platform. The piano sat to one side. Toulouse's backdrop was already set up against the wall. He'd painted it to look like a real stage, complete with a red curtain, but he still needed to add some finishing touches. After the stage was set up, Toulouse opened a jar of red paint and got to work.

Marie and Daisy sat down at a "directors' table" facing the stage. It had everything they needed: paper, pencils . . . and tea and cookies. Marie glanced over a list she'd made, with

The Terrific Talent Show Planning Checklist written across the top.

> *Get names and descriptions of all the acts.* Check.

> *Decide what order they'll be in.* Check.

> *Explain to Berlioz and Toulouse that there should be only one show host.* Check.

> *Give Berlioz and Toulouse other jobs so they won't be too disappointed.* Check.

> *Give Berlioz a list of acts he needs to play music for, and what kind of music.* Check.

> *Make a list of costumes and props for Berlioz and Toulouse to collect.* Check.

> *Plan out the scenery flat for Toulouse to paint.* Check.

> *Write out what the host (me) will say in between each act.* Check.

"Oh, Marie," Daisy said, looking over the list of acts. "Even though your song comes first, I think you should rehearse after everyone else. I'm worried that when the other performers see how great your act will be, they won't feel as confident."

Flattered, Marie nodded. "That makes sense. I don't mind going last." She checked the list of acts. "Pouf? You're up. Are you ready?"

In a flash of fluffy tail and brown fur, Pouf appeared onstage, holding his little sack of acorns between his paws.

"Ready, ready, ready!" he chittered.

Pouf opened the sack and pulled out one, two, three acorns. Then he flicked his tail at Berlioz as the cue to start playing. As the music began, Pouf tossed one acorn into the air, then the second, and juggled them.

Marie whispered to Daisy, "I'm impressed," and Daisy nodded in agreement.

Pouf threw the third acorn into the air. For a moment, he had all three acorns going at once . . . until one acorn flew into another. One landed on the floor and rolled under a table. The other bounced off some piano keys.

"Oopsie whoopsie!" Pouf exclaimed. "Can I try again?"

But on Pouf's second try, all three acorns flew off into different parts of the café.

"Hey, Pouf," Toulouse called. "Maybe you should just do the cheek-stuffing part. And instead of acorns, the audience could give you food from their plates."

Marie glared at her brother. That

was a terrible idea! Pouf's act would become complete chaos.

Fortunately, Daisy spoke up. "We'll keep the juggling, Pouf. Practice makes better! Make sure you get plenty of it before the show."

"I will!" Pouf stammered. "I promise! Lots and lots of practice will make better, better, better!"

Next up was Toulouse with his comedy act. He climbed onstage wearing the red top hat, spectacles, and scarf from Madame's attic—Duchess had let him borrow these.

"Hello, everyone!" he announced. "Did you hear what happened to the cat who swallowed a ball of wool?" After a pause, he grinned and said, "She had mittens!"

Everyone in the room burst into giggles.

Toulouse continued with another joke. "Do you know what to do when a naughty dog chews on a dictionary? You take the words right out of his mouth!"

More laughs.

"Your brother's funny," Daisy murmured to Marie.

If only he'd focus on his own act instead of butting into others', Marie thought.

Berlioz suddenly piped up. "Toulouse, I think I should play a few chords right after you say each punch line."

Berlioz demonstrated on the piano. Toulouse scrunched up his nose. "Thanks, Berlioz. But I don't think I need the music. The jokes are funny without it."

"Okay," Berlioz replied. "But . . . what if, during the show, I play music only if it seems like you *do* need it?"

Daisy leaned in close to Marie. "Berlioz is holding up the rehearsal. You're the director. It's your job to tell him to stop."

Marie nodded and cleared her throat. "Can you two talk about this later?"

Toulouse ignored her. "Why would I need the music?" he asked his brother.

"Are you jealous that I'm doing an act all by myself?"

"Jealous?" Berlioz scoffed. "Not one bit. I'm in a great act of my own!"

"Mrrrrow!" Daisy stood up and put her front paws on the table. "Stop fighting! Berlioz, this is Toulouse's act! And you're not the director. Stop making suggestions."

Berlioz flattened his ears. "I'm sorry," he mumbled as he turned back to the piano. "Go ahead."

Marie felt a flutter of jealousy. As the show director, she should have been the one to get her brothers to stop fighting.

After Toulouse finished rehearsing, he went back to painting the backdrop. Spike went next, rolling all over the stage in time to Berlioz's piano music.

"Hey, Spike!" Toulouse called out when Spike began to slow down. "Can you spin in one place, like a top?"

Spike paused, then started doing what Toulouse suggested. He whirled faster, then faster, and then . . . right off the stage and onto the hard floor.

THUD.

"Ouch!" Spike called out, unrolling himself and rubbing his head. "That hurt. A lot."

Toulouse threw down his brush and came running over. He held up his front foot. "How many paws am I holding up?"

"Um . . ." Spike said, squinting. "I'm not sure. Five?"

"Spike!" Berlioz exclaimed. "Nobody has five paws!"

Daisy gave a concerned sigh and

turned to Toulouse. "Toulouse, can you get Spike some ice for his head? He'll need to rest before rehearsing again."

Marie thumped her tail anxiously against the chair. *Every act has been a total disaster so far!*

Hopefully the next act—Berlioz and the Alley Cats—would go smoothly. Isabel, along with a few other kitties, came onto the stage with their instruments. Marie couldn't wait to hear them all play. But wait . . . what was that squeaky sound?

Marie noticed that the Alley Cats were leaving red paw prints across the stage. She rushed over and followed their tracks to a puddle of red paint on the floor, next to an empty jar.

"Toulouse!" she called out. "You spilled your paint when you ran over to help Spike!"

Daisy came to see, checking out the paw prints from different angles and narrowing her eyes. "Just let the paw prints dry. They'll become part of the set decoration. This one in the middle can be everyone's center stage mark."

"Daisy, you're so good at solving show problems!" Berlioz remarked.

"Yeah," Toulouse chimed in. "I don't think we could do this without you."

Marie felt a huge lump in her throat. It was true. Daisy had done a lot. But her brothers hadn't said anything like that to *her*. *Maybe I'm not doing a good job as director*, she thought.

Finally, the time came for Daisy to

go onstage. Marie hadn't yet seen Daisy practice her monologue. She was very, very curious to hear it.

From the very first line, Daisy wasn't Daisy anymore. She was Julie-cat, telling the audience about falling in love at first sight with a tabby cat named Ro-meow.

"Ro-meow, Ro-meow, where-fur are you Ro-meow?" Daisy said, her voice heavy with emotion.

When Daisy finished, everyone gave her a huge round of applause.

"Okay, Marie," Daisy said as she came back to the table. "Show us what you've got to open this Terrific Talent Show!"

But Marie hesitated. Compared to Daisy's act, Marie's song was nothing special. It was nothing, period.

Chapter 6

The applause for Daisy continued, but
Marie found her courage and walked
onto the stage. She could do this!

Marie tried to step around the red-
paint paw prints. When she reached her
mark, she looked out across the café.
Everyone had been waiting to hear her
sing. Especially Daisy.

Marie spotted Toulouse over in
a corner, holding a bag of ice against

Spike's head. Nearby, Isabel frantically tried to wipe red paint off her clarinet.

Berlioz placed Madame's sheet music on the piano and began playing the first notes of the song. Marie glanced over at him, listening for her cue. Wait . . . what was that on the first page? She leaned in to see better. A bright yellow smudge . . . and Berlioz had been eating a mini quiche earlier.

Marie almost let out a growl of frustration but stopped herself. They'd all promised Mama to be careful with Madame's belongings! What else could go wrong? And why couldn't she fix all these problems the way a true director should?

Marie took a deep breath through her nose and opened her mouth. It was time to start singing.

But . . . she had no idea how.

What's the first line of the song? What's the first WORD?

Berlioz slowed his playing for her to catch up. His expression said, *Come on! Sing!*

Everyone else stared, too. Marie stood still as a statue, alone on the stage.

Finally, Berlioz stopped playing and leaned over. "Marie, what's going on?"

"I don't know!" Marie whispered back.

Daisy approached her, but Marie didn't want to talk to her. Or anyone. The next thing she knew, she was leaping off the stage and dashing into the café's cool and quiet back room.

Marie looked for a place where she could hide and, hopefully, think. She climbed inside the box of props and costumes they had borrowed from Madame, and closed her eyes.

Now all the song lyrics came back to her. Of course they'd been in her head all along.

So why couldn't I remember them?

It couldn't be stage fright. She'd performed for a café full of animals countless times!

But this was different. Marie had never tried to be a theater director before. And instead of sticking with the plan she'd made, her brothers and the other cast members were creating trouble.

What if, when she got up to sing at the performance, she froze again?

The Terrific Talent Show? Everyone will end up calling it the Terrible Talent Show.

A familiar smell rushed over Marie: the delicious scent of sugar and flour, fruit and cream. She loved baking and working in the kitchen. She also loved helping Berlioz with his songs and singing with her brothers. All that had been going well. Why had she ever wanted to try something new?

Marie heard claw scratches at the

door. Two short, one long. Then a second time. It was the secret code that meant her brothers were on the other side.

"Come in," she called, crawling out of the costume box.

Berlioz pushed open the door to the back room, and he and Toulouse crept in. There was red paint on Toulouse's whiskers, and some on Berlioz's paws.

"Marie?" Berlioz said softly. "We're sorry about the paint puddle. Toulouse and I cleaned it up, but we, uh, got some of it on us."

"What happened to you out there?" Toulouse added.

Berlioz swatted at him, getting a bit of red paint on Toulouse's fur. "Be a little more sensitive." He turned to Marie. "Did I do something wrong with the song?"

"Not exactly," Marie began. "I noticed that the sheet music got dirty, after we promised to be careful with it."

Berlioz looked down at the floor. "Sorry. I promise I'll clean it later."

"And you kept insisting that Toulouse's act needed music," Marie added.

"Yeah," Toulouse chimed in. "I know you were just being funny, but that was not okay."

Marie rolled her eyes at Toulouse. "You've been fooling around, too! Making silly suggestions to Pouf and Spike. Spike ended up getting hurt!"

Berlioz and Toulouse exchanged a guilty look.

"There's a reason why you have to plan out a show," Marie continued.

"You have to be organized . . . not silly. Otherwise, it'll be a disaster."

"I'm sorry, Marie," Toulouse offered.

"We'll help you stick to your plan from now on," Berlioz said. "You have Daisy to help, too. And her act is great!"

"It really is," Marie echoed, staring at the floor. "She was also great at dealing with all the problems that popped up. Much better than me."

"Well, she lives in a theater, right?" Berlioz asked. "She's an expert."

"But the talent show was *my* idea," Marie said. "I'm supposed to be the director."

Toulouse's face lit up. "Hey, I have an idea! Maybe Daisy should be the director. That way, you can just focus on your song."

"Toulouse, that's not helpful."
Berlioz swatted his brother again, flicking
more red paint at him. This time it
landed on Toulouse's nose.

"Oh, you're going to get it for that!"
Toulouse shook his head, and the paint
on his whiskers went flying, splattering
Berlioz's face.

Berlioz blinked hard once, then
twice. Suddenly, he was in the air,
tackling Toulouse. They tussled their
way across the floor of the back room.

Marie let out the biggest, angriest
growl she could. *MMMMRRRRROW!*
"Stop it, you two!" she shouted. "Why
can't you take any of this seriously?"

Berlioz stopped kicking at Toulouse
with his back feet. Toulouse stopped
pawing at Berlioz's neck.

"I just wanted to perform Madame's song," Marie said. "Why did I have to put on a whole talent show?"

"You thought it would be fun, remember?" Toulouse replied. "But maybe it's not so fun right now."

Marie thought about that for a few moments. "Then I know what we need to do."

She shook out her tail and ears, then marched out of the room. Toulouse and Berlioz followed her into the café.

Spike was still rubbing the bump on his head. Pouf was in the corner, trying and failing to juggle three acorns. Daisy was running around, picking them up wherever they fell.

Marie jumped on top of the piano

and shouted, "Attention, everyone! I have an announcement!"

All the creatures in the café stopped what they were doing and looked up at Marie.

"The Terrific Talent Show," she said, "has been officially POSTPONED."

Chapter 7

The café grew strangely quiet, and nobody moved.

After a few long moments, Pouf broke the silence. "What? . . . Why?" he asked, slowly and softly. Not Pouf-like at all.

"Because the acts won't be ready in time," Marie said. "This rehearsal was a complete disaster! How can we possibly put on a performance tomorrow night?"

"But we've invited every alley cat in Paris!" Isabel exclaimed.

"Even some nice dogs," Antonio added. "They'll all come to the café, expecting to see a talent show."

"And I'll be going home to London before long," Daisy said. Then she jumped onto the piano and tapped Marie with her paw. "Marie, you're completely new at this. No wonder the rehearsal was a little . . . messy."

"A *little*?" Toulouse blurted out. He snapped his mouth shut, looking guilty. Daisy smiled sadly at Marie, as if she felt sorry for her.

Marie glared at her brother, then glanced at Daisy. From the moment they met, Daisy had seemed like a big sister. Now it felt different between them. As if . . . they were in a contest. And Daisy was winning.

"Please, Marie," Berlioz began. "I've already put up lots of posters to advertise the show. So this rehearsal didn't exactly . . . uh . . . go well. Can't we have another one before the performance?"

"Good idea," Toulouse added. "I'm sure Daisy can help all the acts get better."

"Isn't that why you asked *her* to be your assistant director instead of us?" Berlioz said.

Ouch, Marie thought.

She had expected everyone to be relieved that the show was postponed. Seeing everyone's disappointment made Marie feel a hundred times worse.

"I know you're frustrated," Daisy said. "But we can work out all the

 91

problems. Everyone wants to perform tomorrow. We have a saying in the theater: the show must go on!"

But what if it goes on, and it's awful? It was such an upsetting thought, she didn't want to say it out loud.

"I have an idea," Daisy whispered, leaning in close. "You really want to sing your song, right? Maybe you should just focus on that. I can take over as director, and we can have another rehearsal tomorrow like Berlioz suggested."

"You'd . . . take over as director?" Marie echoed, loud enough for everyone else to hear.

"Excellent idea!" Berlioz exclaimed.

"Yay, Daisy!" Toulouse added.

"Thank you!" Pouf squealed, running in a circle around the

piano. "You're the best! I promise I'll practice!"

Spike rolled himself over to them, then unrolled with a huge grin on his face. "Daisy saves the day!"

As all the other animals began to crowd around the piano to talk to Daisy, Marie backed away. She jumped down to the floor, then crept toward the door. Nobody seemed to notice as she slipped into the alley.

They all love Daisy. Even my own brothers! Much more than they love me.

Then another, shadowy thought crossed Marie's mind as she headed home.

Maybe this was Daisy's plan all along. She seemed so nice and friendly. But maybe she was just acting. What a drama queen!

The next morning, Marie told Duchess she didn't feel well. She curled up in her special sunny spot in Madame's library. A few hours after Berlioz and Toulouse left for the café, Duchess came to check on her.

"You don't have a fever," Duchess said, licking Marie's forehead. "I think you have a case of 'I don't want to be at the café on the day of the talent show.'"

Marie protested, but Duchess gave her a knowing look.

"You're right, Mama," Marie said with a sigh.

"But Daisy encouraged you to sing your song, yes? It's not too late to be part of the show."

Marie shook her head. "I'm sure

everyone's angry with me." Then she remembered how much she wanted to perform Madame's song, especially for her mama. "But I *would* like to be in the show. Grrr, my thoughts are all jumbled up!"

Duchess smiled. "Madame always says the best way to clear your head is to take a stroll outdoors. That's why she loves going to the park."

The park. It was such a peaceful, beautiful place. A perfect place to think.

"I'll be back soon," Marie said, getting up and straightening her bow.

"I'm glad you're feeling better," Duchess said with a wink.

Within minutes, Marie was outside, putting one white paw in front of the other down the sidewalk. She headed in the direction of their favorite park, the

Luxembourg Gardens. But after a few streets, another place called to her. If she remembered the way . . .

Marie sniffed the air. *I think I do remember.*

She set off in the direction her nose told her. Many blocks and a few wrong turns later, there it was: Le Théâtre du Lion Jaune.

The basement window was still open, and Marie squeezed through it. She quietly retraced the steps she'd taken with Daisy. But when she got to the big wooden doors, there was no human there to open them. She *did* hear human voices inside, though. Marie glanced around to see if there was any other way to reach the stage. There was a wide set of stairs leading up to a second floor. It reminded Marie of the grand staircase at Madame's house.

Marie began climbing. When she got to the top, she spotted something exciting. A door had been propped open. She loved when humans did that!

Marie crept through the doorway and suddenly realized where she was: on one of the balconies. She went to the edge and stood on her hind legs, stretching her body as tall as she could. There was a railing there. She grabbed it with two little paws, then peeked over the top.

The stage was down below. And that's where the humans were!

Marie could tell they were rehearsing a show.

Nobody was making a mess.

Nobody was getting hurt. Nobody was even fighting! Marie watched for a few minutes, wishing she could be down there. If she could, she'd ask the actors what it felt like, to perform in front of a big audience. To share their talent with the world.

Then, one of the actors raised his voice. Another actor raised his voice, too. They were having some kind of disagreement. They kept looking at the script and pointing to writing on the page. Marie wondered what was going to happen next. Would they have to go outside and argue? Would one pounce on the other, like her brothers did?

Instead, one of the arguing actors said something and put his arm around the other's shoulder. They both started laughing. Then the other actors started laughing, too.

"They're having so much fun," Marie whispered to herself. She let go of the railing and planted all four paws back on the floor.

A happy memory popped into her head: she and her brothers in Madame's attic, playing around with their discoveries. Another happy memory: sitting at the piano in Alley Cat Parlor, singing while Berlioz, Isabel, and Henri made music to go along with the song.

Marie remembered the moment that happened after that one. *I came up with the idea for the talent show because performing makes my heart dance.*

And performing with her friends and brothers made it dance even more.

She heard a human voice down below, coming from the rows of red velvet seats. Marie peeked over the railing again and spotted a man sitting in the audience.

"Very well, you all!" the man yelled out. Marie could hear him more clearly than the actors. He must have been the director. "I must say, that was terrible!

But we're going to do it again and again until it's better!"

A clock chime sounded throughout the theater. The talent show performance would be starting soon.

In that moment, Marie realized this wasn't the stage she wanted to be on. That was the wobbly one at the café, covered in red paw prints. Where Daisy had held a rehearsal without her.

Maybe if she ran, she'd make it back to the Purrfect Paw-tisserie before it was too late.

Chapter 8

Is EVERYBODY in Paris out and about today?

Marie was a white-and-pink streak as she raced down a crowded sidewalk, veering this way and that to avoid crashing into human legs or a bicycle wheel. She had never seen the city streets so busy.

As she ran, questions whirled in her head. Would everyone forgive her for quitting the show like that? Would they

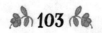

let her come back so she could help them make the show a success—and sing her song, too? Or at least, *try* to sing, if she didn't freeze up again.

She dashed across an intersection of two streets, thinking the way was clear. But a horse pulling a delivery cart came out of nowhere. Marie jumped out of the path of a giant hoof just in time.

"Mrrrow!" she called out, startled.

"I'm so sorry!" exclaimed a dapple-gray horse. "I didn't see you there. Are you okay?"

"Yes . . . but I'm the one who should apologize. I'm in a hurry and wasn't paying attention."

The horse glanced back at his driver, who was talking to another human on the sidewalk.

"Where are you headed? Maybe I can give you a ride."

"Would you?" Marie exclaimed. "I need to get to an alley near the Luxembourg Gardens."

The horse let out a cheerful neigh. "That's right on my way! Hop on! But quickly."

He lowered his head so Marie could climb onto his neck. It reminded her of how Madame's horse, Frou-Frou, often gave the kittens rides through Paris.

"My name's William," the horse said. "Tuck yourself under one of those reins. My driver won't notice you."

"I'm Marie," Marie said as she settled into a good spot. "It's nice to meet you, Monsieur William."

William, she repeated to herself. *Like*

*William Shakespeare, the playwright Daisy
likes! It must be a sign.*

Soon they were near the entrance
to the alley. While the driver stopped to
make a delivery, Marie gave William a
pat and climbed down.

"Thank you very much for your
help," she said. "If you have any smaller
animal friends, send them to the
Purrfect Paw-tisserie. I'll make a special
apples-and-greens muffin for them to
bring you."

William neighed. "I will do that!"

Marie raced toward the café
entrance and slipped quietly through the
door. If the performance had already
started, she didn't want to interrupt.

But inside, the café buzzed with
noise, packed with an audience

chattering among themselves. The stage was empty. Berlioz sat at the piano, fidgeting with his tail.

He glanced up and spotted his sister. "Marie! Thank goodness you're here!"

"What's happening?" Marie asked. "The performance should have started by now."

Berlioz beckoned with a paw and Marie drew closer. "It's Daisy. She refuses to come out and introduce the show."

"Refuses? Why?" That didn't sound like Daisy at all.

"I don't know," Berlioz replied. "Toulouse is talking to her now."

"Maybe I can help."

Marie slinked along a wall of the café, toward the back room. The door

was ajar, and Marie could see Daisy
sitting at a mirror. She wore a flower
crown and trembled with fear. Toulouse
sat next to her.

"I . . . just can't do it," Daisy said.
"I'm too scared."

"But your monologue was amazing
in rehearsals," Toulouse said.

"I didn't have time to practice the
hosting part. And this is the real show,
with a real audience. I've never hosted,
or done a monologue, or performed
anything for a real audience!"

"Wait . . ." Marie said, stepping into
the room. "*Never?*"

Daisy and Toulouse both stared at
Marie in surprise. They were all silent for
a few awkward moments.

Then Daisy shook her head. "I've

always been a behind-the-scenes kind of cat."

Marie couldn't help smiling. "That's funny. Because I've performed for an audience before . . . but never tried to be a director."

Daisy smiled a bit, too. "So we're opposites. It's scary, trying something new."

"Definitely," Marie agreed. "And sometimes harder than you think it's going to be."

Now Berlioz came into the room. "So? Are we going to do a show or not?"

Marie turned to her brothers. "You two were right. I shouldn't have taken all the planning so seriously. This whole idea started because we have fun performing together and with our friends. Sometimes

we come up with new ideas as we go. I was so nervous about directing a show for the first time, I forgot about that."

"Well," Berlioz began, throwing a glance toward Toulouse, "we could have been more helpful with your plan."

"We should have noticed how stressed out you were getting," Toulouse added.

Spike and Pouf poked their heads in the door.

"The audience is getting restless," Spike said. "Some are even talking about leaving."

Marie turned to Daisy. "I think we should introduce the show together. Then it won't be so scary, right?"

Daisy thought about that, then nodded. "Right."

"Then," Marie continued, "if you want to do your monologue at the end, you should. But if you don't want to, that's okay, too."

Marie went over and put her head close to Daisy's. They saw themselves in the mirror again.

"Look at us," Marie said. "Two stars. Not in the future. We're stars *now*. We're trying something new even though it's scary and hard."

Daisy smiled. "I guess that's what stars do."

Marie and Daisy headed out to the café. When they took their places onstage, the audience started to clap.

"Finally!" said a poodle sitting in the front row next to Pierre and Louis.

Duchess and Thomas O'Malley were right there, too. Duchess gave Marie a tiny Mama-always-knows-best smile.

"Welcome!" Marie said. "Here at the Purrfect Paw-tisserie, we believe everyone has a talent."

She paused and glanced at Daisy. Would she say the next line?

Marie watched Daisy take a deep breath, then say, "We're excited to have some of our friends show off theirs today! In the theater, we don't say 'good luck.' We say 'break a leg' instead!"

"So to all our performers . . ." Marie said. "*Break a leg!* Let's start the Terrific Talent Show!"

"First, we have someone who's . . . already here onstage!" Daisy beamed, with no trace of stage fright. "Here's a kitty who's a baker, a café manager, a songwriter, a singer . . . and my good friend. Marie!"

The audience barked, meowed, chittered, chirped, and squeaked. Daisy stepped offstage as Marie found her mark. Berlioz sat down at the piano and smiled at Marie. In the wings, Toulouse tipped his top hat at her.

As Berlioz started playing, the notes filled Marie's heart. The sight of Duchess in the audience, beaming with joy, lifted her spirits further.

This time, the song lyrics were right there, ready to burst out. She opened her mouth and began to sing.

Hello to the sun, hello to the sky
Hello, warm breeze as you pass me by. . . .

Marie lost herself in the lyrics, which made her feel like she was telling the story of spring to everyone listening. When she sang the last note, the audience exploded in applause. She took a bow, imagining herself onstage at Le Théâtre du Lion Jaune. She'd done it. And it was just as wonderful as she'd hoped it would be.

After the applause died down, Marie introduced Pouf and stepped offstage. *Please let everything go perfectly*, she thought. *I'd even settle for "not a total disaster."*

A few moments into his act, Pouf dropped two of his acorns. But instead of getting flustered, he just said, "Oops! They're slippery today!" The audience laughed, and he tried again. By the time he took his bow, he'd juggled all three acorns for a full minute and set a new personal cheek-stuffing record.

"Bravo!" Marie called to Pouf as he left the stage, impressed that he'd turned his mess-up into a joke.

Next came Toulouse in his hat, spectacles, and scarf. From the moment he did that silly walk onto the stage, everyone in the café was giggling. At the end of every punch line, Berlioz played a few funny-sounding piano chords. They must have figured this out during the second rehearsal. *I'm impressed*, Marie thought.

Spike's rolling routine went perfectly. No falls, no bumps. He got a standing ovation.

When Berlioz and the Alley Cats played, the audience started to dance. It felt like the entire Purrfect Paw-tisserie was bouncing! Marie felt her fur puff up when some chairs and tables got knocked over. One of Toulouse's paintings fell off a wall.

It's okay, Marie told herself. Nothing was broken. Nobody was hurt.

Antonio stumbled a few times during his dance. But he covered it up by turning the stumbles into new steps. Marie and Daisy exchanged a glance; the audience didn't know that anything had gone wrong.

Finally, it was time for Daisy to perform her monologue. Marie noticed she was trembling again.

"Remember," Marie whispered to her friend. "You're doing what makes your heart dance. That's all that matters."

Daisy nodded. "Thank you," she said . . . then stepped onstage.

The calico kitty from London wowed everyone with her acting. After she finished, all the performers went up to take a final bow together. It took a long time for the applause to die down.

With the show officially done, Duchess and Thomas O'Malley rushed over to give lots of nuzzles to Toulouse, Berlioz, and Marie.

"My darling kittens!" Duchess exclaimed. "You were all simply wonderful! I'm so proud!"

"But next time you almost get caught

in the attic," Thomas O'Malley added,
"I'm not covering for you."

As the kittens laughed, Duchess
turned to Marie. "The order of the acts
was perfect."

"Thank you, Mama," Marie replied.
"Not everything was perfect, though."

"No . . ." Duchess said. "But
imperfect is so much more interesting,
don't you think?"

Marie felt a paw tap her shoulder. It was Daisy.

"Thank you, Marie," Daisy said. "You helped make my first trip away from home a real adventure! I hope you can visit me in London. And now that you have experience, I hope you do more shows at the café."

"Me too," Marie replied. "Someday, when you're starring in your own play, I'll be watching from the front row."

Daisy and Marie hugged. After Daisy stepped away, Marie spotted a piece of paper stuck to the wall between the piano and the backdrop: her checklist! Some items had been added to it in Berlioz's and Toulouse's handwriting.

"We continued your planning during

the second rehearsal," Berlioz said, stepping up beside Marie.

"It did make things easier," Toulouse added as he joined his littermates.

Marie took a glance around the Purrfect Paw-tisserie. At the knocked-over tables. At a few acorns Pouf had left on the stage. At a tiny red-paint paw print on the floor. Then, at all the different types of animal audience members chattering happily, and the performers beaming with pride.

"Organization is definitely good," Marie told her brothers. "But when you're putting on a show . . . I'd say that mixing in a few spoonfuls of chaos makes the best recipe.

Jennifer Castle is the author of over a dozen books for kids and teens, including the Butterfly Wishes series and American Girl's Girl of the Year: Blaire books. She lives in New Paltz, New York, with her family, which includes five cats and, often, a few rescued foster kittens, who are all likely planning their own creature café when the humans aren't looking.

Sydney Hanson is a children's book illustrator living in Sierra Madre, California. Her illustrations reflect her growing up with numerous pets and brothers in Minnesota, and her love of animals and nature. She illustrates using both traditional and digital media; her favorites are watercolor and colored pencil. When she's not drawing, she enjoys running, baking, and exploring the woods with her family. To see her latest animals and illustrations, follow her on Instagram at @sydwiki.

All-New Illustrated Chapter Books Inspired by Disney Classic Movies

AVAILABLE NOW!